STORIES

This is a work of fiction. All names, characters, places, and incidents
are the product of the author's imagination. Where the names of
actual people, places or corporate entities appear, they are used for
fictional purposes and do not constitute assertions of fact. Any
resemblance to real events or persons, living or dead, is coincidental.

Cover design and typesetting by Geoffrey Bunting
Cover image by Dave Glass

ISBN 978-1-967756-06-3

First Edition

Published by Otis West
OtisWestBooks.com

Author's Note

I wrote these stories in my early twenties—between 1990 and 1994—while living in Palo Alto, Iowa City, and San Francisco. For years, they existed only on a floppy disk, half-forgotten in the back of my desk drawer. They are presented here in their original form—time capsules from a bygone era.

STORIES

OTIS WEST

Rocks

Seth and I are down in the gully behind his house with some of his model cars and a packet of firecrackers. It's a bright fall day and all the trees are turning colors. You can just see the roof of Seth's house over the top of the rise.

Seth is kneeling, pushing firecrackers into the windows of an orange Corvette. He also has a white Daytona, but it's the Vette he really wants to blow up. His father owns a real one, and the last time Seth saw his father, he was driving away in it.

Seth shoves two more firecrackers into the front wheel wells and connects them all with one fuse. It's like he's the pro and I'm an apprentice or something, even though I've done this a million times. But this is Seth's ditch, and these are Seth's models, so I just stand and watch.

When he's done, he turns to me and smiles. "It's ready."

He lights the fuse and stands back. They go off one after another—fast and loud—and the car leaps into the air and the doors blow off. A last one goes off and the sound comes back at us from the hillside. Blue-gray smoke rises from the car and the air smells like sulfur and burnt plastic.

I say, "Cool," but Seth doesn't say anything. He has a vacant look on his face. He stands over the smoldering model a second and then he steps on it. There's a loud crack as the car sinks into the leaves and the wheels pop off. When Seth picks up his foot, the hood and roof are caved in. He steps on it again, and then again, and when he looks at me, he has this weird expression on his face, as if I had caught him doing something. His nose and ears are red with the cold.

"Ever lit one of these in your hand?"

And before I can answer, he does. He just stands there, smiling and clenching the firecracker in his fist. He makes a grimace, and it goes off, dull. He shakes his hand and laughs. Then he says, "Your turn."

I say, "No," but he hands me a firecracker and the lighter.

"Come on, it feels cool."

I'm holding the firecracker in one hand and the lighter in the other and Seth's watching me. It's like he and all the fall colors are in my face, crowding in on me. I light it and hold it away, just like Seth did.

Seth says, "Don't let go," and he laughs.

The wick is smoking and spitting and getting shorter, and just before it goes off—just as I can feel the heat—I tighten my grip and close my eyes. I feel the jolt in my arm and the noise. My ears are ringing and my hand seems suddenly larger, expanded—I can feel the space between each finger.

Seth is laughing and I'm staring at my hand. At first there's a dull, throbbing ache, but then my hand starts tingling like hell. It's like my hand is asleep, but the tingling shoots all the way up to my funny bone and it hurts. I start to feel dizzy and for a second I think I'm going to puke.

Seth stops laughing and then he's just looking at me. He says, "What's wrong?" and then he walks up and grabs me.

"What's wrong?"

His face is all twisted up like he's angry or concerned—I can't tell which.

I say, "It hurts, okay," and I end up yelling the "okay" part. I can feel water pooling around my eyes.

Seth lets go of me, almost pushing me back. "Fuck, man," he says. He picks up the Daytona and says, "Come on." He starts walking up the hill toward his house.

Inside, his mother and ten-year-old sister are on the living room couch, watching TV. His mother doesn't let her eyes drift from the screen, but his sister stares at me as we walk past. She's got her legs folded up under her like she's a duck or something. She's always like that—not moving, not saying anything, just staring. I put my hand in my pocket and follow Seth to his room.

When his father moved out, Seth's mom started sleeping in the same room with Seth and his sister. It freaked Seth out, so he moved into the basement. He switches on the light and closes the door behind us as we head down the stairs.

The room is large, but there is almost nothing in it. Just a couch, Seth's bed, his father's old stereo, and a big red carpet. One wall is a bookcase, stacked with old National Geographics. A few weeks ago, a cricket crawled in behind them and Seth and I spent almost an hour pulling all the magazines off the shelves until we finally found the thing and killed it.

There is a back area with a work bench and a large sink. Seth told me that his father has to come back some time because he left all his tools. I walk back there and turn on the faucet.

My hand is still tingling but it's more numb than anything. I hold it under the cold water for a while, and when this doesn't do anything, I turn the water on hot. Steam starts coming out, but I can't feel anything except where the hot water splashes onto my arm.

I pull my hand out and look at it. It's pinkish red, and when I feel it with my other hand, the skin feels thick and soft. It feels like something that's dead.

I start to think about what my parents will say and about the hospital and I want to cry. I stand there for a moment and hold my breath.

When I come back out, Seth is sitting on the couch, smoking a cigarette. "How is it?" he says.

I just shrug, and Seth says, "It must have been a faulty one or something." Then he says, "Sorry."

I don't want to sound like I'm still freaked out about it, so I don't say anything. I sit on the floor across the room.

After a few minutes, Seth gets off the couch, walks over to me, and hands me the cigarette. Then he walks back over and sits on the floor, too. He leans back against the couch.

"You probably shouldn't go home for a while," he says, letting out the smoke he has been holding all this time. "'Til it gets better."

I nod and let the smoke fill my lungs.

Seth has a phone in his room. I call my parents while he goes upstairs to tell his mother that I'm staying for dinner. My older brother, who's in high school, answers. "What'd you do?" he says.

"Nothing," I say. I can hear my parents laughing in the background.

"Sure," he says, and just as I'm about to say that I didn't do anything again, I hear him yelling to our parents, saying that I'm going to stay over at Seth's. My brother is always like that—messing with me just enough to show that he knows what I'm up to.

"They want you home by eight," he says. "You okay?"

"I'm okay." I know I can trust my brother, but I'm too embarrassed to admit what happened.

"Sure?" he says.

"Sure."

Dinner is cold leftovers—chicken and rice. M*A*S*H is on TV—a small black and white sitting on an old baby chair. We all watch.

Seth's sister keeps staring at me. When I stare back she blinks, but she keeps staring. I look back at my food. I'm not even hungry.

Seth's mother eats one piece of chicken, and then she just sits back, smoking. She taps the ashes onto her plate. She has fat, flabby arms and a weird way of clenching her jaw when she blows smoke through her nose. I remember when I first met her and how she used to go out of her way to ask me how I was doing and how my parents were doing—even though she only met them once. I guess that I've been around her too much now. She doesn't seem to notice me anymore, just like she doesn't seem to notice Seth.

When Seth finishes, he gets up and says, "Let's go."

I pick up my plate, rinse it, and put it in the dishwasher. My parents have drilled this into me. I feel lame doing it—like I'm uptight about manners—but it's a habit.

When I turn around, I see that Seth has been watching me from the doorway. When our eyes meet, he looks away and walks back to the table. He gets his dish and puts it in the dishwasher. Then he starts putting in everything from the sink—plates, cups, and handfuls of silverware. He does it violently and it sounds like he's going to break something. He takes his mother's plate and then his sister's—she holds onto her last piece of chicken—and puts them in, too. He bends down, pours in too much detergent and slams the door shut. Then, with his fist, he punches the buttons. A red light comes on and with a whirring sound the dishwasher starts up.

His mother, who had been watching him the whole time, gets up and takes an ashtray off the windowsill. She sits down again and looks back at the TV.

Seth looks at me and says, "Okay?"—like he's mad at me.

I say, "Okay," but he's already walking out of the room.

When we get back to Seth's room, he says, "Well, what do you want to do? Your hand's still fucked up, right?"

I say, "Yeah," and because Seth is being a real asshole all of a sudden, I say, "Don't worry about it."

"Fuck, man." He shakes his head and looks at the floor.

I don't know who's making a bigger deal out of this anymore, me or Seth. I say, "I should just go home."

Seth's doesn't even look at me. He says, "Come on," and heads back up the stairs.

Seth has a moped he stole out of someone's backyard. He told me that it had been sitting there for over a year, that whoever owned it was just letting it rot. He repainted it, bought new tires, and got it running again. The muffler is busted and the whole thing starts to shimmy at about thirty, but it still runs okay.

It's a clear night and all the stars are out. I'm holding onto the cold metal behind the seat and my hands are so cold that I almost forget which one is screwed up.

After a few blocks, Seth starts fucking around. He's slowing down and speeding up and weaving the bike around. I know that he's doing this just to piss me off, so I try to ignore it. But then he starts leaning way back, almost pushing me off. I say, "Hey, quit it."

Seth glances back at me and then we're veering off the road. I hold on tight as we go into the gravel and then alongside a ditch for a while, running over ruts and stones so the moped is shaking and jumping all over the place. We head back through some trees and onto the street again, bouncing hard as we hit the pavement. Seth brakes to a stop and jumps off—pushing me off the back. He dumps the moped and runs into the woods on the other side of the road.

It's weird how quiet it is. The streetlight is right over me, so I have all this yellow light in my face and I can't see anything past it. It's like I'm on stage or something. I yell, "Seth!" but he doesn't answer.

I start to pick up the moped, but then there's a loud clank against the gas tank and I hear Seth laugh. Then a rock hits me in the shin.

"Shit!" I say. It stings like hell. When I step forward, another rock hits me in the leg. Two more skip past me.

"Asshole," I say, but not very loud—it doesn't come out right.

I'm waiting for the next rock when Seth walks back into the light. He's tossing a rock lightly in his hand and he has this weird smile on his face.

"What's wrong with you?"

Seth doesn't say anything. He walks right up to me, still tossing the rock.

"What?" I say.

"What?" he says, mocking me.

"Fuck you," I say.

"Ooh," he says. "Big boy said a bad word." He twists up his face. "My hand hurts. Take me home to my mommy and daddy."

"At least I have a dad." As soon as I say it, I regret it.

Seth pushes me, hard. I stumble and fall backwards over the moped.

"You're just a little shit," he says. "You're just a pussy momma's boy." His fists are clenched like he wants to fight, but then I see the tears. He wipes his nose and looks away.

I stand up but he's already pulling at the moped. He says, "Come on," and I help him get it back up. He gets on and starts it, and when I don't get on right away, he says, "What?"

But I'm just looking at him.

"Nothing," I say.

When we pull up in front of my house, my brother is in the garage, lying under his car with a flashlight. His legs are sticking out and I can hear the metallic hiss of his walkman turned up loud.

As I slide off the back of the moped, Seth says, "How's your hand?"

I say, "Fine," but I'm not even thinking about it. The lights are all on in my house and long shadows are splayed out across our front lawn.

The engine starts to rattle and sputter like it's about to stall.

Seth says, "See you later."

I say, "Yeah," and then I run across the front grass toward my house. Just as I reach the front door, I hear the engine choke and quit. I turn to see Seth trying to kick start it. I stand there a second more, and then I go inside.

When I get past my parents and up to my room, I look out the window to see if Seth is still out there. At first I think he's gone, but then I see him—way down the street, pushing his moped home.

Get Away From Me

My dad got a new girlfriend and so I was supposed to be friends with her kid. He was only thirteen, but he tried to act all cool, wearing baggy pants and a baseball cap turned backwards. And he was always at my house, like he thought he lived there or something.

At first, I made the mistake of being nice to him. I even took him to a party at my friend's place. He hung around me the whole time, trying to act like he knew how to smoke a cigarette—except he was blowing smoke through it. Little orange sparks were shooting out the end.

"You're doing that wrong," I said.

He didn't seem to care. He just smiled at me.

I came in late one night, and my dad had Ellen up against the kitchen counter. His pants were around his ankles.

I said, "Jesus Christ, dad." I don't think he even heard me.

When I got to my room, I found the kid sitting on my bed, flipping through my porno mags.

"What the fuck?" I said. "Get out of here."

But the kid didn't move. He had this look on his face that freaked me out. It was like he thought I was crazy—like I was the one with a problem.

That was it. He could have my room. He could have everything. I went out to my old Datsun and drove away.

I moved in with a friend. The next day, my dad called.
"Why don't you come back? We miss you."
"Who's we?"
"Me, Ellen, and Jason."
"I don't give a fuck about Ellen and I don't give a fuck about Jason."
"Oh, come on," my dad said. "You didn't even give them a chance."
"What?" I said. "What?" I held the receiver away and looked at it. More words were coming out, but I couldn't hear them, could understand them. I hung up.

That kid was haunting me. Everywhere I went, I'd see kids who dressed and looked just like him. He even started popping up in my dreams—with those baggy pants and that stupid hat. It was scary.

A week went by. My dad called again.
"What do you want for your birthday?"
"It's not my birthday."
"Isn't it coming up soon?"
"No," I said. "Try in a few months." I hung up.

I wouldn't have gone back but I needed some clothes. I went incognito and borrowed my friend's Mustang.
I parked across the street. I was about to get out of

the car when I saw that kid sitting on our front porch. It was like he was guarding the place.

And then his mom came out, followed by my dad. They were walking right toward me—like one big happy family.

I ducked down. They didn't see me and they didn't look when I started the engine. Just as they were crossing in front of me, I floored it.

The tires squealed and spewed blue smoke (my car could never have done that) and the three of them ran.

When I was halfway down the block I slowed down and looked in the rearview mirror. My dad was comforting Ellen on the sidewalk. But that kid was standing in the middle of the road. He was looking after me like he knew what was going on, like he knew that it was me—and I think he did.

Two weeks went by, and then my dad called again.

"I'm not coming back," I said.

"But she's gone," he said. "It's over."

He told me how she'd gotten weird on him—how she had wanted to get married, and how when my dad said no, she locked herself in the bathroom and threatened to kill herself.

"What about the kid?" I said.

"I didn't like that kid," he said. "He was always around."

So I moved back home. It was weird at first, but then it started to feel normal again. What can I say? I tried not to think about it too much.

A few weeks later I was watching TV when my dad came in. He was freaked out.

"She's here," he said.

"What?" I said. "But I thought..."

"Turn off the TV. I don't want her to know anyone's home."

I shut off the TV. My dad and I crawled across the living room floor on our hands and knees. Then, slowly, my dad pulled back the curtains.

There she was, standing on the front step, ringing our doorbell. She stood back and put her hands on her hips.

My dad turned to me and whispered, "Where do you think that kid is?"

A chill ran up my spine. Suddenly, my mouth was dry.

"I don't know," I said. "But I bet he's around here somewhere."

Hit and Run

Eddie and I were driving around, trying to think of something to do. We had been smoking pot and watching TV at his house when his sister came home with her boyfriend and kicked us out. So now we were circling around town, with my mom's old Buick stalling out at stoplights.

"What do you want to do?"

Eddie shrugged. "Fuck if I know." He was sitting with his feet up on the dashboard. It was a summer evening, and the air flowing through the open windows was warm and sweet-smelling.

"Want to go to a movie?"

"No."

I didn't mind just driving, but it seemed better to have a purpose. Or maybe it was better not to have a purpose— maybe it was better to just drive around.

All of a sudden, Eddie sat up. He looked inspired. "Turn here," he said.

"Where are we going?"

"You'll see," he said. "Take another right."

We were heading down a residential street when Eddie said, "Stop here," and jumped out of the car.

I said, "Where are you going?" but he just smiled and ran up the front walk of a small gray house. He knocked on the door and turned to look at me. And then the door opened and he was gone.

I turned off the engine and sat back to wait.

* * *

I woke up disoriented. I was still in my car, but what time was it? How long had I been sleeping?

I heard voices. And then I made out two dark shapes in the middle of the lawn. I got out of the car.

"He's awake," Eddie said.

I heard a girl say something, and then Eddie said, "I was going to wake you up, but Sara said you looked cute with your mouth open."

He stood up and the girl got up after him, brushing grass off her dress.

"So where are we going?" I said.

We were crammed into the front seat. The girl—who Eddie knew from his church group—was sitting between us, chewing gum. She was fourteen, maybe fifteen, and she smelled like suntan lotion.

"Ask Sara," Eddie said.

Sara shifted the gum over to the side of her mouth and said, "Let's go to Jill's house."

"Who's Jill?" I said.

"Sara's fat friend," Eddie said.

Sara punched Eddie in the arm. "Fuck you."

"What?" Eddie said. "She is."

Sara looked at me. "Can you tell him to shut up?"

Jill lived at the end of a cul-de-sac. Several kids were circling around out front on BMX bikes.

Sara rang the doorbell, and after a few moments, Jill came to the door. Eddie was right. She was fat.

The two girls grabbed each other's arms and Sara yelled, "I've got to tell you something!" They turned and ran into the house.

Eddie and I closed the door behind us and went into the living room, where Jill's mom and little sister were watching Star Trek.

Her mom was in her bathrobe, smoking cigarettes. She barely glanced at us when we sat on the thick shag rug, but the little sister wouldn't stop staring at us.

After a while, Eddie said, "What are you staring at?"

The little girl turned red and looked down at the floor.

The next time I looked around, Eddie was gone. I watched TV a while more and then I got up to find him.

I walked into a hallway. The door at the far end was closed, but I could see light at the bottom. I knocked and someone said, "Yeah?"

I opened the door. Sara and Jill were sitting on the bed with their shoes off.

"Where's Eddie?" I said.

"I don't know," Sara said. "Probably jacking off somewhere."

Jill giggled and put a pillow over her face.

Then Sara said, "Are you guys, like, best friends?"

"I guess."

"Do you spend a lot of time together?"

"What do you mean?" I said.

Jill snorted from behind the pillow, and then Sara laughed.

I could feel my neck getting hot. I said, "Whatever," and walked out of the room.

I found Eddie in a room that had been built off the back of the house. It had been set up as a fitness room—with an exercise bike and a bench press.

"What are you doing?"

"Nothing," Eddie said. He was sliding more weight onto the bar.

"Want to take off?"

"Not yet." Then he said, "Spot me," and lay back.

Eddie was on the wrestling team, and he could lift twice his weight. I watched the veins bulge on his neck as he strained with each repetition, and I thought about what Sara had said, and about fat Jill, and I closed my eyes because I didn't want to be there and I didn't care. I knew that someday I would be far away from all of this.

After a while, the side door opened, and Sara yelled, "Hey Eddie, you asshole!" Jill laughed and then the door slammed shut.

"I'm gonna split," I said.

"You are?" Eddie said. "Just hold on one sec." He ran back into the house.

I got in my car and let it idle for several minutes. And even though I knew it was useless, I honked the horn.

Time was nothing. I could wait forever and not care. I waited some more—until someone rode past on the bicycle, the small light weaving slowly down the street—and when Eddie still didn't show up, I backed out and drove away.

* * *

My mom's boyfriend had blocked the driveway with his Bronco, so I had to drive half-way down the block before finding a space.

I was almost back to my house when I heard a screech followed by a loud impact. I turned to see that a pickup had side-swiped a parked car down the street. There was a flash of reverse lights as the guy backed up. Then he got out to check the damage.

I crossed the street and walked back toward him. He looked up at me as I approached. He was about thirty and wearing an oil-stained baseball cap. I could tell that he was drunk.

He said, "It's not yours, is it?" It was like he was accusing me.

"No," I said.

"Shit," he said. "Some job I did."

The car's front door and fender were badly crushed, and the pavement was littered with broken bits of orange plastic from the truck's turn signal. They looked nice under the streetlight—like candy. I felt like picking them up and putting them in my pocket.

He looked at me. "I guess I should leave a note?"

"I guess so."

"You wouldn't happen to have a pen or a piece of paper on you?"

I said no.

"Shit." He scratched his head.

I shrugged and walked back across the street. I didn't look back, even when I heard him get into his truck and start the engine. I was happy to let him go his way—to forget the whole thing.

Phillipe and the Flatulent Dog

Phillipe and I are walking along. Phillipe is angry about his girlfriend. I'm just walking, looking around a bit.

"Damn," he says. "Damn, damn, damn, damn."

We're both wearing sneakers. Converse. They tread the pavement lightly.

"I can't believe it," he says. "I really can't." He kicks an old hot dog bun.

I stop. Phillipe stops, too.

"What?" he says.

"You gotta mellow out."

"I am," he says. "I'm mellow."

"No you're not." I start walking again, not wanting to make too big a deal out of it.

Phillipe catches up with me. He puts his hands in his pockets. "Wanna play some pool?"

"Alright," I say.

Pool makes things worse. My game is on. Phillipe's is off.

"Damn," he says when I win again.

"You suck tonight," I say.

"I know," he says, picking at the end of his cue stick. "Another game?"

"Alright," I say. I rack them up. "You break."

Phillipe eyes the cue ball. "I've got to beat you once."

"You can do it," I say.

When Phillipe breaks, the cue ball shoots off the table and hits the wall. Several people turn to look at us.

"Damn," he says.

It's late when we get out of there. It was late before we went in, but now it's even later. Fewer cars are out and the stars are more present.

"Stars," I say.

"Yeah," he says. Then he says, "Where are we parked?"

"Over there." I point, but when I look where I'm pointing, I change my mind. I turn and point in the other direction.

"You sure?" he says.

"Sure," I say.

My car is a 1963 Plymouth Valiant. Slant six, push button transmission. 280,000 miles on the original engine. The thing glides.

We get in and Phillipe rolls down the window. The handle falls off in his hand.

"Put it in the glove compartment," I say.

Phillipe opens the glove compartment and stuff falls into his lap—a flashlight, some old batteries, the other window handle.

"Be careful," I say.

Phillipe gets everything stored away. Then he slumps down in his seat.

I start it up and push D for drive.

We climb the stairs to Phillipe's apartment. Phillipe tries several keys before he realizes the door isn't locked. When he pushes it open, it jams on the rug. We have to squeeze our way past.

Phillipe takes off his jacket and hangs it on a hook by the door. And then he sees what I've already seen: his apartment mate, Fred, is sitting at the kitchen table with his girlfriend—Phillipe's girlfriend, that is—Felicia. Felicia is sitting on Fred's lap.

Phillipe clears his throat like he's about to say something important. Then he turns to me.

"Beer?" he says.

"Sure."

We walk past Fred and Felicia to the refrigerator. Phillipe pulls out two beers.

"Here," he says, and hands me one. He looks at Felicia again, then back at me.

"Come on," he says.

We go to the living room, which starts where the linoleum ends. The TV is on and Fred's dog is napping on the couch.

We sit on either side of the dog, open our beers, and turn our eyes toward the TV: David Letterman.

After a while, Phillipe says, "He's not funny anymore."

It's true. In ten minutes, I laugh once or twice, but that's it. Then the band comes on and I'm done with my beer.

"I'm gonna split," I say.

"Alright," Phillipe says. He's watching the band. Fred and Felicia have disappeared into the bedroom.

I stand up. "Take it easy."

"You too."

I look at the dog for a moment. Its eyes are closed. It is breathing heavily. I sense that my timing is perfect.

"Adios," I say.

Outside, it's about the same. Streetlights. Lots of stars. Maybe the street is a bit wider, I'm not sure.

I walk to my car, open the door, and get in. And then I just sit there—tapping the steering wheel, looking out.

Trick Knee

Beth's car was a piece of shit, rattletrap Subaru with torn-up seats and a rear window made out of a plastic sheet and duct tape. Her father had given it to her. He was one of those hobby guys—retired with too much time on his hands—and this car had been a project of his. He'd rebuilt the engine, done some brake and front-end work, but the whole thing was cockeyed. Anyway, the car had died again—the third time in a month—so we were stranded alongside the highway, calling AAA. I didn't know if it was the alternator or the fuses or the fuel pump and I didn't care either. Let the experts handle it.

Beth and I were talking again, at least. Things had been pretty rocky ever since we'd moved in with her father a month before. We had planned to stay with him until we had jobs—until we could afford the deposit for an apartment—but it was taking too long to save the money and Beth's dad was starting to drive me nuts. In any case, we'd just spent a very pleasant day at the beach, but then I'd ruined the mood with some rash, unguarded statements about her father, and for the last twenty miles of freeway she'd been giving me the silent treatment. But when the car gave out she went into crisis mode, which made communication critical. Within seconds of pulling over, she had formulated a plan. Now she had me lighting flares while she talked on the roadside telephone.

There is nothing worse than standing alongside a California highway at night, backed up against a cement wall with drivers careening past four cars abreast. I was standing amongst the debris—retreads, smashed batteries and cigarette butts, underwear and shoes. It was too easy to imagine what would happen if someone wasn't paying attention, if someone let their car wander a second. You see that shit all the time—a car drifting onto the shoulder before the driver corrects.

Before I met Beth, I had never broken down alongside the road. I'd always driven big American cars that ran. Cars built in the 60s and early 70s that you didn't have to think about. The closest I'd ever come to being stranded like this was with some friends in high school when we ran out of gas. We were on a long downhill, stoned out of our minds, when the engine cut out. In the silence, we'd had a long time to contemplate what was happening. But then, as if by magic, an exit appeared, and then a gas station. We coasted in—the big neon sign swinging overhead as the last bit of momentum got us up the curb and alongside the full-service pumps.

So I'd been living this dreamy, charmed existence, coasting. And then I met Beth and started breaking down on the freeway.

I lit two flares. There were more, but I decided to save them for next time. I got back in the car, shutting the door on the noise outside. The flares made this weird pinkish smoke that drifted around in the night air, and the flashers beat a steady pulse against the railing.

I watched Beth, who had just hung up the receiver. Her shoes had gotten wet at the beach, and so she was tiptoeing back to the car, barefoot. She was oblivious to the cars rushing past. It was this same nonchalance that allowed her to live in the same house with her father. I felt like I was the only one aware of that huge semi careening toward us.

She walked up to the front of the car, waited for a break in the traffic, ran and got into the driver seat.

"They said about fifteen minutes." She looked at me and then gave me a kiss. "I'm sorry."

I didn't know if she was talking about the car or about our general situation. I said, "Me too."

The big beams were on us. I sat up and squinted. It took a good minute or two for the guy to get out of the cab, and then I saw why. He was probably three or four hundred pounds. But it was weird—he was probably in his thirties, but he looked like a little kid. Like a big fat little kid.

He had the baseball cap, the blue shirt with "Jim" embroidered on the pocket, the clipboard with the pen tied to it with a string. He asked some basic questions, did some perfunctory paperwork. I thought he'd do more to find out what the problem was, but I guess he didn't really care. Why would he? So he asked where we wanted it towed. Beth gave him her father's address, and we got into the cab while he hooked up the car.

The whole truck tilted as he climbed into the cab. He was breathing heavily. He started up the big diesel and we were off.

I was scared that he'd try to strike up a conversation, but he didn't. He cleared his throat, rolled down his window a bit, and glanced over at Beth, who was dozing on my shoulder. I smiled and closed my eyes, too.

His radio kept going off. Half asleep, I listened to the voice of the dispatcher. The night was filled with people who had broken down, who were stranded along the highway. We were safe, above it all.

We turned onto Beth's father's street, to the end of the cul-de-sac, the headlights sweeping across the front lawns of the surrounding houses. I had been hoping that her dad wouldn't be home—which was stupid, because he never left the house—but the lights were on.

We piled out, and the guy walked around back to undo the harness. He was breathing pretty hard. Beth headed up the front walk. I was trying to decide whether or not to follow when the guy fell over backwards and rolled into the bushes.

Beth turned around and said, "Oh my god."

I walked over to him and said, "Are you okay?"

The guy was breathing hard. He seemed to be resting—nudged up against one of the junipers that Beth's dad was always watering. It was also a favorite shitting place for the neighbors St. Bernard.

After a moment, he said, "I'm fine. It's just my trick knee."

He rolled back over, then got up—slowly, pushing himself up with his good leg. He limped part-way back to the harness, and then he fell over again.

I laughed that time—I couldn't help it. But I felt bad. And when I glanced at Beth, she gave me a look.

This time he took even longer getting up. He was breathing heavily.

I heard the front screen door slam shut, and when I looked around, I saw the silhouette of Beth's father walking toward us.

The guy sat up. It sounded like he was hyperventilating.

Beth knelt down and said, "Do you need some help?"

The guy didn't answer right away. He pulled up his pant leg, revealing a knee brace. Then he said, "I think I pulled something."

Beth's father had joined us without a word, in his bathrobe and slippers, his silvery hair shining in the moonlight. He looked at me, and then at Beth and said, "What's going on?"

Beth said, "This poor man hurt his knee."

Beth's dad frowned. He was the sort of guy who would be thinking about the legal ramifications of having someone splayed out on his front lawn.

The guy started to get up, but then sat back and shook his head.

Beth's dad leaned forward, and, as if he was talking to a small child, said, "What can we do for you?"

The guy didn't answer right away, and I didn't blame him. Finally, he said, "I just need to rest here for a moment."

He needed to rest for more than a moment. Beth's dad went inside and called AAA, told them they had a man down, that they should send someone to pick him up.

Beth, meanwhile, had gotten some blue ice packs together. She seemed disappointed when he didn't want them.

"I could use a smoke, though."

I had a few cigarettes left, so I gave him one, lit it, and then sat down to join him. Beth was watching us.

"I'll be there in a minute," I said.

Beth gave me a weird smile, then turned back toward the house.

It was a nice evening out. I was glad to be out here on the lawn, not inside with Beth and her father.

After a while, the guy said, "I'm gonna lose my job."

"Can't you sue them or something?"

He seemed to think about this for a moment. Then he said, "I don't think so."

"Did you hurt your knee on the job?"

"No. But it's been making it worse."

"They can't fire you for that."

"There are other things."

I nodded. I felt like I knew what he meant. There were always other things.

I glanced back at the house. With its windows ablaze, it stared back at me.

I turned back to see that the people across the street had pulled back their shades to get a look at us. I suddenly felt a surge of hate toward these people, toward everyone in this neighborhood.

"What are they looking at?" I said.

"Me, I guess."

I flipped them off.

The guy laughed.

A while later two guys showed up in a tow truck. They were younger than our driver—a bunch of hot shots. One of them helped the guy into the truck while the other kid disconnected the Subaru.

"So what was wrong with this thing?" the kid said, when he was done.

"I don't know. It just cut out."

The kid got in, leaned down under the dash and did something I couldn't see. Then he started it up, and got out, shaking his head. "It was just a fuse." He laughed and got in the guy's truck. "That guy is a loser."

I watched as he backed out and drove away, and then I got in the Subaru. The engine was running fine—better than ever, it seemed.

And suddenly I knew that this was it—it was a sign. I honked the horn. I waited a moment and then honked again. I'd give her two minutes, and that was it.

The porch light was on, but the rest of the house was dark. I sat there and waited. I watched for movement.

My New Place

I found this new apartment—a studio—and moved in. A couple times a day this siren goes off. I can't figure out if it's a car alarm or what.

"It's an ambulance," Carl says.

Carl came over to help me get my couch up the stairs. Now we're just sitting around, drinking beers.

"How do you know?" I say.

"Ambulances make that sort of noise these days. So you won't mistake them for something else."

"But it always comes from the same place, and it doesn't move."

"You got a hospital around here or something?"

"I don't think so."

Carl takes a sip of his beer. "I don't know, man. I think it's an ambulance."

Before I found this place, I was living in a house with my girlfriend Sheryl and some of her friends. They were always hassling me about my truck, saying that I was hogging the garage. It was getting so that Sheryl was siding with them.

Carl comes back from the kitchen with two more beers. He hands me one, then cracks open the other.

"So when's Sheryl gonna see this place?"

I ignore the smirk on his face and say, "Who knows."

Carl nods, but then he starts laughing.

"What?" I say.

"Nothing."

"Fuck you. What?"

"Nothing," he says. "I said nothing, okay?" He looks down at the floor, his mouth twitching as he tries to quit smiling.

I take another sip from my beer. "Whatever."

After Carl leaves, I sit around some more, just looking at the place.

Besides the couch, I've got a few vinyl chairs and a futon. Otherwise, the apartment is empty except for the roach motels that were here when I moved in. They're these little black hexagons with a hole on one side, and they're all over the place. I keep stepping on them.

My neighbors get home a short while later. First their light flashes into my kitchen, and then their music comes on, loud—I can feel the bass through the floor.

So I decide to go over to Sheryl's. I can't call because my phone isn't hooked up yet.

* * *

Sheryl's room is in the middle of the house. There aren't any windows—there's just this plexiglass skylight that used to drip water on us when it rained.

It's weird to be over there. She's already rearranged her stuff—she's got it spread all over the room, in places my stuff used to be. It makes me jealous in a way. Jealous of the room.

She says, "So, are you all settled in over there?"

"Pretty much," I say. "Carl helped me."

She says, "Uh huh," and picks up this stuffed panda she's had since she was a little kid. She starts pulling at its ears and pushing its fur around.

Then she says, "I should go to sleep."

"Oh," I say. "Okay." And I wait for a moment, to see what happens.

"Well, goodnight," she says.

Her housemates all look at me as I walk to the door. They're watching TV—the one I fixed for them twice. I'm glad to be out of there.

* * *

Carl comes back to my place the next day, straight from work. He sits on the couch and starts pulling beers out of the twelve-pack he brought with him.

He hands me a beer and says, "Here you go, dude." Then he sits back and opens his.

After a while, I say, "I went over to Sheryl's last night."

"How'd that go?"

"I don't know. It's kind of weird."

"What do you mean?"

"I don't know." And I shrug because I don't want to talk about it. I don't even know why I brought it up.

Carl takes a sip from his beer, then sits forward and gets this serious look on his face. "Well, you got a good set up, man. You should be happy."

"I guess."

When Carl goes to the bathroom, I pick up the phone to see if it's working yet. There's a faint gurgling sound and some weird clicking noises, but no dial tone.

Carl comes out of the bathroom just as I'm putting down the receiver.

"Who you calling?"

"Your mom."

"Yeah," he says. "I know who you were calling."

"Who would that be?"

Carl smiles, but then he just shakes his head and cracks open another beer.

We finish the twelve-pack and then work our way through the beers leftover from the day before. By the time we're done with those, it's past two, so it's too late to get more. But then I remember something.

"I've got a bottle of white wine somewhere."

"Oh yeah?"

"Yeah," I say. "I think it's Sheryl's."

I rummage around in a few boxes and finally find it—some cheap stuff with a twist top.

Carl laughs. "Cool."

The wine tastes bad after the beer.

"It should have been cold," I say.

"Yeah," Carl says. He winces with each sip.

I take one more drink, and then I pour it into the sink.

Carl says, "Damn," and does the same.

Carl ends up crashing on the couch, so I give him my old army jacket to use as a blanket.

Later, when I get up to take a piss, I look at him. He's curled up like a little baby.

* * *

When I wake up, the apartment is filled with daylight. Carl is still asleep on the couch.

I go out on the fire escape to smoke a cigarette and watch people on the street below. I flick ashes down at a few of them, but no one seems to notice.

Then I think to try the phone. When I pick it up, I get a dial tone.

So I call Sheryl.

She says, "Did you just call and hang up?"

"No," I say. "Why?"

"Oh," she says. "Never mind."

I wait a moment, and when she doesn't say anything else, I say, "Want to come over? Check out my place?"

"Not today."

"Well, how about tomorrow or something?"

"I don't know."

"What?" I say. "Oh, come on."

There is another silence, and I picture her sitting in

her room, staring down at her brown carpet. Or maybe she's picking her toenail or something.

"Fine," I say, and hang up.

And then I'm the one looking at one of those little roach motels. I pull it apart to see if it's caught anything, but there's only this white powder that gets all over my hands.

And then that car alarm—or ambulance or whatever the fuck it is—goes off, and Carl wakes up and starts looking around, his face all messed up from sleep.

He says, "What's going on?" and he looks at me, like I have any idea.

John's Dad

John called me in a panic—he needed to pick up his dad at the airport, but his truck wouldn't start.

"You loser," I said. It was getting late. My girlfriend and I had been watching TV and we were about to go to bed.

"Come on, man. I'd do it for you."

"You would?" I said.

There was a pause—he was fumbling with the phone—and then he said, "What?"

"I'm on my way."

"Thanks, man. I owe you."

I pulled up in front of John's place—a converted garage set back from the street. John had been living there ever since we finished high school, all the time saying he was going to quit his job at Safeway and move somewhere else.

I walked in to find him sitting cross-legged in the middle of the floor, trying to repair a cassette tape. He had unraveled about twenty feet, looking for the kink.

When he saw me, he said, "Can you hold this a second?"

I took the cassette and he started pulling out more tape.

"This thing is like a fucking möbius strip."

He kept pulling out more and more tape. Just as I said, "You're going to rip it," the tape broke. John grabbed the cassette out of my hand, balled it up and threw it across the room.

For a moment, neither of us moved. I could hear the phone ringing in the house next door.

"So, we going?" I said.

"Yeah." John stood up and started feeling his pockets. "Do I have everything? Where's my wallet?"

We drove for several blocks before I realized I hadn't turned on the lights. The dash lit up as I pulled the switch.

John hunched forward and started rubbing his arms like he was cold. "What time is it?"

"I'm not wearing my watch."

John said, "Oh." Then he said, "Could you turn on the heat?"

"It's on," I said. "You just can't feel it yet."

As we merged onto the freeway, John said, "I'm not looking forward to this."

I wasn't either. I hadn't seen John's dad in years—since before his second wife had left him. He had just spent the last week with John's sister in LA, seeing some sort of lung cancer specialist. John had told me that he had less than a year to live.

John slumped down in his seat. "I hope I got the information right."

We got to the gate as the last people were coming off the plane.

"Shit," John said. He dropped himself into one of the molded plastic chairs.

"Maybe we should check the baggage claim area."

"Yeah." He stood up. "Okay."

A red light started flashing and the conveyor belt stopped, leaving only a bag of golf clubs and a mangled cardboard box.

John was pacing back and forth. "Maybe I fucked up. Maybe he's coming tomorrow." He fished around in his pocket until he came up with a crumpled piece of paper. "I should call my sister."

I followed him to the phones. Just as he started talking to the operator, a hand reached from behind us and tapped John on the shoulder.

We turned around to see John's dad, who was wearing scratched-up aviator glasses. His sweater was inside out and he reeked of whiskey.

"Hi Dad," John said.

John's father shook his head. Then he walked over to a garbage can and spit out a chunk of phlegm.

"Nice," John said.

John's father sat in the back seat. I opened my window, but as soon as we got on the freeway, he started complaining he was cold. I rolled my window back up, but he kept complaining.

John said, "Yeah man, crank up the heat."

"I told you, it's on," I said. "It's just that the blower's busted."

John frowned and turned to look out the smudged passenger-side window.

John's father coughed. I could feel his knees pressing into the back of my seat.

John's father still lived in the house where John had grown up—just down the street from my parents' old house.

We were halfway up the front walk before John's father realized he didn't have his house keys. He stopped, opened his suitcase and spilled the contents onto the lawn—a mess of dirty laundry and a bunch of pill bottles.

"What the fuck?" John said. "What are you doing?"

John's father didn't answer. He was pushing his stuff around and muttering.

"Dad," John said.

John's dad wouldn't look at him, wouldn't say anything. He shoved his stuff around some more, and then he walked over to the front step and sat down.

John said, "Come on," and nodded for me to follow.

We circled the house, looking for an open window. We were walking close to the house, getting snagged by bushes and stumbling across water spigots and drainpipes. And then John tripped on the gas meter and fell. For a while, he just sat on the ground, holding his shin. "I don't believe this," he said. I thought he might be crying, but in the dark, I wasn't sure.

We finally found a window that was open, and I gave John a boost. And then he was inside, turning on lights.

I didn't want to be hanging around John and his dad anymore, so I walked around to wait on the front step.

The house next door had the TV blaring, and all the lights were on. Big Wheels and bicycles were scattered across the driveway.

When we were kids, an old widow had lived in that house. She used to turn on the sprinklers and forget about them, so that water would flood the street. John's mother always sent us over to shut them off. We'd sneak over there scared—sure that the old woman was watching us. I wondered what those kids with the bikes and Big Wheels thought of John's dad.

I didn't see John until he was standing in front of me.

"Let's get out of here."

John didn't say anything all the way back. He just slumped in his seat and looked out the window.

I said, "You warm enough? Want me to turn up the heat?" but he didn't laugh.

I pulled up in front of John's place and shifted into neutral. No one was around. The street was dark and quiet.

John got out, then leaned down to look at me.

"Take it easy," he said.

"You too."

He frowned. "Sorry about all that bullshit."

"Don't worry about it."

John shrugged and looked down the street. The engine had dropped into a low idle, and exhaust was piling up in the red glare of the taillights.

How old were we then? Twenty-two? Twenty-three? I was gone by the time his father died—my girlfriend got pregnant and then we moved down to LA—so that was probably one of the last times I saw John. I remember looking at him and getting a chill—like I was already looking back on this, like I was already miles and years away.

John slapped the side of the car. "Alright, man."

"Alright," I said. "See ya."

"Yeah."

I watched as he headed up the driveway and disappeared around the side of the garage. Then I eased it back into drive and pulled away.

Back

My brother Dan lived on the first floor of a three-story apartment complex. The sprinklers were on in front and water was running across the sidewalk and into the street. By the time I reached his door, my sloppy wet footprints had faded into the district crisscross patterns of my Converse.

I rang the doorbell and waited. After a minute or so, I heard a scratching sound as my brother undid the chain to open the door. And then he was standing there, wearing just shorts and tube socks. Behind him, a large orange cat leapt off the couch and started meowing.

"Hey," I said.

Dan smirked, then stood back to let me in. I walked into the small living room and dropped my duffel bag in the middle of the floor.

Dan shut the door, then walked past me and into the bathroom. The cat tried to follow him in but backed out as my brother closed the door.

I hadn't seen my brother for over three years—since we had been living with my mother. At that time, he had just quit his job to go back to school. I had just dropped out of college and wasn't doing much of anything. This made me a low-life in his opinion. He was always giving me shit, telling me what I should do.

One night, we got in a fight, which I can only remember in parts. I left the next day.

A lot had happened since then—Dan got married, my mother remarried and moved away. And me? Let's just say that for a short while things had worked out—I was living with a girl I loved and working at a decent job. But then everything fell apart. The girl moved back in with her husband and I lost my job. For the past few months I had been sleeping on the couches of people I barely knew. So now I was back. There were some things I had to figure out.

Dan got a can of cat food out of the cupboard. He popped it open and squatted down to spoon the pink meat into the cat's bowl. He said, "Jen should be back soon."

Jen was his wife. I remembered her vaguely from high school—I remembered her being tall and stuck up. I hadn't been invited to the wedding, so this would be the first time I would have seen her in four years.

Dan came back into the front room and sat across from me on the couch.

"You've got a cool place."

"Yeah," he said. "It's alright."

I could hear the cat chewing its food—eating so fast that it was almost gagging.

I said, "What's the cat's name?"

"Stanley." Then he said, "He has leukemia."

"What?" I said—and I laughed. "How do you know?"

"The vet told us. He's going to die soon."

I looked back at the cat, which was still gulping down its food.

Dan said, "Want a beer or something?"

"No thanks."

He shrugged, then picked up the remote and switched on the TV.

Jen was nothing like I remembered her. She had dyed black hair and too much makeup. She closed the door before she saw me.

"This is Colin," Dan said, standing up. "You remember."

She nodded and smiled like she remembered—even though I'm sure she didn't. "Oh yeah," she said.

Dan and Jen sat on the floor, and Jen massaged Dan's neck. They talked to each other in low voices—saying things I couldn't make out over the TV. From time to time she'd look at me and smile.

I listened to them having sex in the next room. The cat walked around me purring. It smelled like cat food and, I thought, disease. When it jumped up onto the couch, I pushed it away.

* * *

The next morning I drove across town to see our old house. My mother had sold it to two old homosexuals and my brother had told me that I would barely recognize it.

He was right. They had cut down our old Sycamore and set up a rock garden. And what I didn't notice at first was that they had changed the color—painting bright blue over the yellow color I had grown up with. I got out of the car and walked around the side.

No one was home, so I climbed through the bathroom window. I knocked over a bunch of pill bottles as I fell onto the tile floor.

The house was different on the inside, too, with new paint and wallpaper, with different furniture. They used my mother's bedroom as the master bedroom—the floor was littered with men's shoes—and they had turned my brother's room into some sort of study. And my old bedroom had been converted into a fitness room, with a weight set and a wall-size mirror.

I went into the kitchen. There were new cabinets, stocked with vitamins and spices and herbal teas. The fridge was filled with diet food. I pulled out a yogurt with NutraSweet in it. I found a spoon, and I was about to sit down when the phone rang.

I walked into the living room and listened while the machine picked it up. Hearing a strange voice broadcast through the house made me feel like some kind of ghost.

Whoever it was hung up, and there was the sharp burst of the dial tone, which was replaced by a dull hiss and mechanical clicking as the machine reset for the next call.

I took a bite of the yogurt, but it made my throat hurt. I tossed it out and got out of there.

* * *

I was watching TV when Jen walked in. She was wearing a miniskirt, which made her legs look like sticks.

"Oh hi," she said.

"Hi."

She went to the fridge and pulled out a jar of cold water. She poured herself a glass and turned to me. "Want some?"

"No thanks."

She screwed on the lid and put the jar back in the fridge.

I watched as she flipped through the mail she had brought in, and I suddenly got the feeling that I was making her nervous, that she was scared of me. It was weird. It made me feel scared, too.

She threw some junk mail in the trash and then she went into the bedroom and shut the door.

That night, I woke up and couldn't remember where I was. I heard voices outside, and then a car's headlight moved across the walls of my brother's apartment like a searchlight. It was like a warning. I made up my mind to leave.

* * *

From then on, I slept in my car. And I started keeping an eye on the men who lived in our house.

One guy was fat and the other was skinny—like Abbott and Costello. Costello would leave every morning—squeezing himself into his little Civic—and Abbot would leave about an hour later in his big Bronco. I had no idea where they went or what they did, but they would be gone the whole day.

So I started spending time in my old house. It was cold and quiet during the day, and after a while, it was easy to forget that someone else lived there. As the sun got low in the sky, the thermostat would click on, and the furnace would roar to life, blowing heat into the house.

Sometimes, I'd call my brother's place. If he answered, I would hang up. But if Jen answered, I'd talk to her until she made some excuse to get off the line.

I felt like I needed to set things straight—like I needed to explain myself. It was just a matter of waiting for the right moment—of waiting to know what it was I had to say.

Some cops woke me up one night—shining flashlights on me and asking me to step out of the car.

There was something cold and familiar about their faces. I felt that I could trust them, and I wanted to tell them everything, but I also knew that it wouldn't be what they wanted to hear. So I told them that I was fighting with my girlfriend, and I gave them my brother's address. They apologized for waking me up and then they left me alone.

Once, I was talking to Jen when my brother came on the phone. He said, "Why are you calling us all the time?"

"All the time?"

"Yeah," he said. "Why?"

"I don't call all the time." As I said this, I remembered the fight we had two years before—I remembered the look on my brother's face as I pressed my knee into his chest.

"Where are you?"

I had to put my hand over my mouth to keep from laughing.

"Is this supposed to be funny?"

Before I could think of an answer, he hung up.

It was maybe an hour later, while I was watching TV, that Costello came home. I shut off the TV just in time, so he didn't hear me, didn't know I was there. I heard him move through the house—down the hallway, dropping his keys on the hall table, and into the kitchen. I waited a moment, and then I got up.

He was sitting at the kitchen table, eating one of those diet yogurts. He just kept spooning the yogurt until he was done, and then he spent a long time scraping the inside of the container with his spoon, like he could get something more out of it.

It made me think about what my brother had said about the cat. He's going to die soon.